THE
RUNT

Other Fat Albert Titles Available in Yearling Books:

ELIZABETH LEVY is the author of many books for children, among them the Something Queer series *(Something Queer Is Going On, Something Queer at the Ball Park, Something Queer at the Library,* and *Something Queer on Vacation).* Ms. Levy grew up in Buffalo, New York, and now lives in New York City, where she writes full-time.

BILL COSBY, well-known comedian, recording artist, concert performer, and television and screen star, has achieved international recognition for his hilarious commentaries on growing up. Born in Philadelphia, he attended Temple University and received his Master's degree and his doctorate in education from the University of Massachusetts. He lives outside of Amherst, Massachusetts, with his wife and five children.

YEARLING BOOKS are designed especially to entertain and enlighten young people. Charles F. Reasoner, Professor of Elementary Education, New York University, is consultant to this series.

For a complete listing of all Yearling titles,
write to Education Sales Department, Dell Publishing Co., Inc.,
1 Dag Hammarskjold Plaza, New York, N.Y. 10017.

THE RUNT

Adapted by ELIZABETH LEVY

A YEARLING BOOK

Published by
Dell Publishing Co., Inc.
1 Dag Hammarskjold Plaza
New York, New York 10017

This book is published by special arrangement with
Eric Lasher and Maureen Lasher.

From the Filmation TV Script
written by LEN JANSON *and* CHUCK MENVILLE

Yearling® TM 913705, Dell Publishing Co., Inc.

ISBN: 0-440-47538-4

Printed in the United States of America

First printing—April 1981

Series design by Giorgetta Bell McRee

FL

THE
RUNT

Chapter One

PEE WEE GETS THE BALL

Fat Albert and the Cosby kids were about to choose teams to play basketball. Fat Albert was captain of the Shirts, which meant his team kept their shirts on. Bill was captain of the Skins, which meant his team wore no shirts. Their pet duck, Cluck, stood in the middle of the court.

"Move, Cluck," said Weird Harold. "I need space." Weird Harold flipped a bottle cap into the air. "Call it, Bill," he said.

"Heads!" shouted Bill.

The bottle cap hit the ground and everyone bent over to see what it was. Cluck tried to peck at it. Weird Harold picked it up from under Cluck's beak.

"It's heads," he announced. "Bill gets first pick."

"I pick Weird Harold," said Bill. Harold smiled, happy to have been chosen first. He walked over behind Bill.

As they chose up sides, Pee Wee, whose name barely gave credit to the smallness of his person, walked up and stood shyly to one side. He watched for a moment and then finally gathered up the courage to speak. "Can I play?"

"Who said that?" Fat Albert looked around, but he missed Pee Wee, because Pee Wee only came up to Fat Albert's knees, and Albert was looking up, not down.

Pee Wee tugged on Albert's trouser leg. "Me, down here."

Fat Albert finally looked down. "Oh, sorry, Pee Wee, but we got enough guys."

"Yeah," said Rudy, laughing. "But if we need somebody that's two foot three, we'll call you."

Pee Wee walked away. He slumped down by the fence and watched. Fat Albert's team played great all afternoon. The sky began to turn a deep blue, and it was almost dinner time. "Hey, hey, hey," announced Fat Albert. "You Skins don't stand a chance against us, no way."

"The game's not over," shouted Bill. "Keep your shirt on."

"Okay," said Fat Albert, and he started dribbling down the court. When Fat Albert dribbled, the whole earth shook.

Rudy, who was on Fat Albert's team, maneuvered himself down under the basket. "I'm free! I'm free!" he shouted. "I got a great shot. Come on, Albert, quit hoggin' the ball and pass it."

Fat Albert passed the ball, but with so much force that it slammed into Rudy's stomach. Rudy slid around the court like an out-of-control hockey player, then finally slowed to a stop, his eyes rolling. He handed the ball to Fat Albert and walked off, clutching his stomach.

"Hey, Rudy, where are ya going?" asked Fat Albert.

"Home," answered Rudy weakly. "I don't feel so good." Rudy staggered down the street, leaving Fat Albert's team one player short.

"Guess we can't play anymore," said Fat Albert. "It's getting late anyhow."

"I can take Rudy's place," said Pee Wee.

Everyone looked down. A big smile spread over Bill's face. With Pee Wee on Albert's team, maybe the Skins would have a chance. "Yeah, Pee Wee," said Bill, "that's a great idea. C'mon, Albert, let's play. Pee Wee is on your team."

Fat Albert looked down at Pee Wee. He looked so anxious to play that Fat Albert didn't have the heart to say no. "Okay, Pee Wee," said Fat Albert. "You can be a forward. There have been lots of great forwards who were short."

"Thanks, Albert," said Pee Wee. "I won't let you down." Pee Wee dribbled down the court. He was so small that every time the ball bounced up in the air he went up with it. Suddenly, Bill snatched the ball from his hands, leaving Pee Wee sprawled on the ground. Bill drove for the basket and made an easy lay-up.

Fat Albert helped Pee Wee off the ground. "Sorry, Albert," said Pee Wee, "I really blew that one."

"Don't sweat it," said Fat Albert. "We're still way ahead."

But Fat Albert spoke way too soon. In the next five minutes, Pee Wee made every mistake possible on a basketball court. Whenever the ball was passed to him, he was knocked over. And the bigger kids stole the ball from him time after time.

Slowly the Skins ate away at the Shirts' lead until they were only two points behind. Fat Albert had the ball. He was dribbling down the court when somehow Pee Wee managed to run underneath him. Fat Albert tripped, dropped the ball, and toppled to the ground. The whole earth seemed to vibrate as Albert lay on his back like a turtle, his arms and legs suspended in midair. Bill grabbed the ball and made a basket.

"That ties the score!" shouted Bill happily. Bill ran back to help the other kids, who were trying to lift Fat Albert to his feet.

"You all right, Albert?" asked Russell.

Fat Albert stood rather shakily. "Hey, hey, hey," he said, but without his usual enthusiasm.

Pee Wee walked slowly away, his head bowed. "Hey, Pee Wee," shouted Albert, "where you going? The game isn't over yet."

"Aww . . . I can't do anything right," said Pee Wee. "I'm too small."

Fat Albert put his arm around Pee Wee's shoulders. "You can't quit now, man. The score's tied. Pee Wee, you can do it."

Pee Wee looked up at Fat Albert for a moment. A spirit of hope lit up his face for a second. "Okay," said Pee Wee, "I'll give it one more try."

Pee Wee shuffled back onto the court. Fat Albert passed the ball to him, and Pee Wee dribbled down the court with a look of fierce determination on his face. Bill ran up and grabbed the ball, but Pee Wee refused to let go, and he wrapped his arms and legs around the ball. Pee Wee was so light that Bill just picked up the ball and Pee Wee too.

Bill shot the ball toward the basket with Pee Wee still holding on. The ball missed and bounced off the rim, but Pee Wee ended up jammed into the basket with both feet sticking straight up in the air.

Weird Harold grabbed the rebound and shot the ball straight toward the basket, where it bounced off Pee Wee's head.

"Goaltending! Goaltending on Pee Wee!" shouted Bill, jumping up and down.

Even Fat Albert had to agree that no member of his team should sit *in* the basket. "I guess you're right," said Fat Albert. "You win."

As the Skins shouted happily, a tear ran down Pee Wee's cheek. Fat Albert helped him down from the basket. "Come on, Pee Wee, cheer up," said Fat Albert. "We all make mistakes sometime."

"Yeah," said Pee Wee sadly. "But for bein' so small, my mistakes are sure *big*."

"You can say that again," said Bucky. "It's your fault we lost the game."

Fat Albert turned around. "Lay off of Pee Wee," he said. "Just 'cause he's small don't mean nothin'. He can do lotsa things you guys can't do."

"Yeah? Like what?" challenged Dumb Donald.

"Yeah? Like what?" echoed Bucky.

"Like tie his shoes without bendin' over," said Weird Harold. "Pee Wee can do *that* with no trouble."

The gang all laughed except Fat Albert. Pee Wee clenched his fist and glared at the gang. Suddenly he wheeled around and tore down the street. He ran up the steps of his house and disappeared through an old, battered pet door.

The kids who had been teasing him looked down at the sidewalk, feeling guilty.

"Now look what you clowns have done," said Bill. "Pee Wee can't help it if he's small."

"Yeah," said Fat Albert. "Pee Wee's cool, so why don't you guys let up on him and try bein' his friend for a change?"

Chapter Two

THE CHALLENGE

The more Fat Albert thought about Pee Wee, the more he decided to take his own advice. He could understand how Pee Wee felt. Fat Albert had never had the problem of being small, but he knew about feeling bad because of your size. Kids had made fun of him too, until he learned to laugh at himself.

The next day Fat Albert went off to find Pee Wee. He took with him a baseball bat, two mitts, and a football. As he walked down the street, he was joined by

Cluck, who waddled beside him. They came upon Pee Wee sitting on the front stoop of his apartment building, his chin in his hands.

"Hey, hey, hey," said Fat Albert. Cluck quacked.

"Hi, Albert," said Pee Wee with a sigh. "What's up?" But it was clear from the tone of his voice that Pee Wee was way down.

"You and I are goin' to play some ball," said Fat Albert.

"Naw, I'm no good at it," said Pee Wee. "Besides, I'm tired of being laughed at."

"Nobody's gonna laugh at you, because nobody's gonna be there except you and me. Man, here's your chance to get in some practice and find out what you're good at."

"I already know what I'm good at," answered Pee Wee. "Messin' up."

"Look," said Fat Albert, "everybody makes mistakes and everybody's good at something too. Let's find out what your specialty is."

Just then Kathy came walking down the street. Kathy was one of Cluck's favorite friends, and Cluck waddled up to her, quacking a hello.

"What are you doing, Fat Albert?" she asked.

"Pee Wee and I were going to do a little practicing to find out what he's good at."

Pee Wee blushed.

"Can I watch?" asked Kathy.

"Only if you promise not to laugh," Pee Wee said.

They walked to a vacant lot between two tenement buildings. Fat Albert gave Pee Wee his bat. Unfortu-

nately, Fat Albert's bat was made for a *big* person, which
nobody could deny was exactly what Fat Albert was.

Pee Wee struggled to lift the bat, but the best he
could do was to rest it on his shoulder. Fat Albert
walked up onto a pile of junk that he always used as a
pitcher's mound. "Here comes the windup," said Fat
Albert. He was in the middle of his windmill motion
when suddenly he stopped, his arm freezing in midair.

"Hey, Pee Wee," he shouted. "Hold that bat off your
shoulder. You'll never get a hit holding it that way."

Pee Wee was too embarrassed to tell Fat Albert that he could barely lift the bat. Fat Albert's pitch whistled past him. The ball rebounded off a wall behind Pee Wee and bounced off the bat before rolling to a stop.

Kathy had to cover her mouth in an effort to stop laughing, and even Cluck seemed to be silently laughing. Lying on the ground, Pee Wee turned to them. "What're you laughing at? I got a piece of it, didn't I?"

Fat Albert hurried over and helped Pee Wee up. He gave Kathy and especially Cluck a mean look. "Don't worry about these clowns, man. We'll just forget about the batting practice and try some pitching."

Fat Albert put on his mitt and crouched in a catcher's squat. "Okay, Pee Wee, put one right over the plate!"

Pee Wee put on the other glove. He slammed the ball into his mitt a couple of times, and then he went into an elaborate windup, a proud expression on his face.

He let go. The proud expression on his face changed to acute embarrassment. He looked down at his left hand. No mitt. He looked down at his right. He still clutched the ball.

Fat Albert was still crouched behind the plate, but he had caught Pee Wee's hurled mitt, not the ball.

There was a sudden roar of laughter from the back fence. All the guys from the gang had found them and come to laugh.

"Try again, Pee Wee," said Fat Albert. "Just move in a little closer."

Pee Wee pitched again, and the ball barely rolled across the plate.

"Move a little closer," said Fat Albert encouragingly.

Pee Wee kept moving in, but his pitches remained feeble. Finally, when they were practically toe to toe, Pee Wee said, "It's no use, Albert. I'm just not a pitcher."

"Let's face it," jeered Weird Harold from the fence, "there's only one position we have for Pee Wee—shortstop."

Everyone on the fence laughed again. Even Kathy laughed. Fat Albert didn't know what to do. Albert knew that with everyone laughing at him, Pee Wee would never get over the feeling that he wasn't good enough just because he was short. Fat Albert felt that there had to be *something* that Pee Wee was good at, but Pee Wee was too discouraged to try.

Suddenly a football came sailing past the guys on the fence, thrown so hard it nearly took their heads off. As the gang ducked, they heard the sound of loud laughter.

When they looked around, they saw five guys from the roughest part of town. They all wore leather jackets and had toothpicks sticking out of their mouths.

"How 'bout that?" said the leader. "I almost got me seven turkeys with one bullet."

Fat Albert stepped up to a hole in the fence and tossed their football back to them. "Hey, you guys are interrupting our baseball practice."

"What's all this jive about baseball? We're here to discuss a *man*'s game—football!" The leader tossed the football casually in the air, flipped it, and deftly caught it.

"So, discuss, man, discuss," said Weird Harold.

"Look here, man," said the leader of the rough gang. "We hear you guys think you're some kinda *bad dudes*. We'll challenge you to the football championship of the world."

A second gang member stepped up close to Fat Albert. "Yeah," he snarled. "Be at Thirteenth and Madison in one hour . . . or we'll hafta come and getcha!"

Before Fat Albert could answer, the leader looked down at Pee Wee and said, "Bring your mascot along. Maybe he'll bring you luck. You'll need it."

The guys in his gang all burst into laughter. They turned on their heels and sauntered away.

Bill, Rudy, Weird Harold, and the others sat on the fence and watched them go. The Cosby kids looked worried.

"Man, those guys are tough!" said Bill. "We don't stand a chance."

"They challenged us, though, so we gotta go through with it," said Rudy. "Don't we?"

Fat Albert nodded. "We'll look like cowards if we don't go," he said.

"We can lick 'em!" said Pee Wee, still steaming with anger over being called a mascot.

"What do you mean, 'we,' " said Weird Harold. "Man, you can't go. You wouldn't last five minutes with those guys."

"Yeah," said Mushmouth, "you're too short."

Furious, Pee Wee gritted his teeth and kicked Albert's football, which was lying on the ground. He started walking away without even looking where he had kicked it. The ball soared through the air as if it had wings.

"Hey, hey, hey," shouted Fat Albert. "Pee Wee, don't go away!"

Pee Wee trudged down the street. He stopped and looked back. He couldn't believe what he was hearing.

"Wow! What a kick!" cried Rudy.

Bill hopped down off the fence and held out his hand to Pee Wee. "Pee Wee, my man, welcome to the team!"

"Do you really mean it?" asked Pee Wee, grinning from ear to ear.

"Do we mean it? Man, if you can kick like that during the game today, we're going to win!"

Weird Harold looked at the clock on the library. "Hey, we don't have much time. I'm goin' home and get ready."

"Me too," said Fat Albert. "Pee Wee, we'll meet you at Twelfth and Madison."

The gang took off in all directions, leaving Pee Wee alone with Kathy and Cluck.

"What about you, Pee Wee?" said Kathy. "Aren't you going home to get ready too?"

Pee Wee picked up the football and began kicking a dent in the ground with his heel. "There's plenty of time to get ready," he said. "I've got to make sure that wasn't just a lucky kick." Pee Wee set the football upright in the dent and stepped back.

"Clear the area!" he warned. Kathy and Cluck moved back. Pee Wee ran at the ball and kicked it as hard as he could. Kathy and Cluck looked skyward.

"Wow!" cried Kathy.

Cluck quacked.

"Pee Wee . . . it wasn't just a lucky chance. It was skill," said Kathy.

Unknown to Pee Wee and Kathy, the tough gang were spying through the cracks in the wooden fence.

"Hey, that little dude can really kick!" cried one of the gang members.

"Those sneaks!" said the leader, slamming his fist into his open palm. "They're trying to pull a fast one by bringin' in a ringer. That little shrimp is probably an all-state kicker."

"What we gonna do?" whined one of the tough guys. "With that little expert kicking extra points for them, they might win."

The gang leader got a sudden nasty smile on his face. "Don't worry. We're going to bring a secret weapon of our own."

"Secret weapon?" asked the second-in-command. "What secret weapon do we got? Are we going to kidnap that little twerp?"

"No," grinned the leader. "I got a better idea." He whispered into his buddy's ear.

"Oh, *that* secret weapon!" smiled the tough kid. "That's cool, man."

The leader turned to his gang. "Let's go, you guys. We gotta couple of things to take care of before the slaughter—" he laughed when he realized what he had said—"I mean, the *game*, this afternoon!"

The tough guys all laughed, but it was a very nasty laugh.

Chapter Three

INTRODUCING KONG!

When the Cosby kids reached the corner of Twelfth and Madison, things did not look so bad for them. The tough gang did not look so tough without their leather jackets.

"Hey, hey, hey," said Albert. "I think we've got a chance."

"We are going to be the *champions*," said Rudy.

"Especially with Pee Wee kicking extra points," added Fat Albert.

"Don't get overconfident," warned Bill. Fat Albert nodded as he took charge. "Come on. We've got to figure out some strategy for our first play." Albert knelt in the street. The other kids huddled around him. He diagrammed pass patterns on the asphalt, using bottle caps, rocks, and pieces of glass to represent the various players.

The leader of the tough gang swaggered out into the middle of the street. "Fat Albert," he shouted, "are you guys ready for your clobbering?"

"You mean winning!" corrected Fat Albert. "Give us a minute."

"Okay," said Albert, "we're going to score on the first play." He slid the bottle cap over to one side. "Russell, you're the bottle cap, see?"

Russell complained. "I don't want to be the bottle cap. I want to be the piece of glass."

"Yeah," said Weird Harold. "And it's my turn to be a rock."

The whole team began to chime in, with each guy shouting out what he wanted. Fat Albert couldn't even hear himself think.

"QUIET!" he shouted. There was instant silence. "Awright," continued Albert. "I'm the captain, so listen up."

Pee Wee was standing next to Fat Albert. He tugged on his shirt. Fat Albert looked around, and then finally down at Pee Wee.

"Whadda you want me to do, Fat Albert?" Pee Wee asked.

"Hike the ball to me, Pee Wee. You'll be center. Then just try to get down the field."

"Okay," said Pee Wee.

The Cosby kids broke out of their huddle, all clapping their hands.

"Ready, one, two, three, hike!" shouted Albert.

Pee Wee centered the ball as hard as he could, but it still fell three feet short of the quarterback, and it bounced along the ground. Luckily, Fat Albert grabbed it on the second bounce, but by then two linemen from the opposing team were charging down on him.

Fat Albert started to run. The leader of the tough guys tried to tackle him, but Albert kept running with the leader holding on to his leg.

"Hey, hey, hey, outa my way!" shouted Albert.

Soon the entire opposing team was hanging on to Fat Albert's arms, legs, and back, but nothing could stop him until he crossed the goal line.

"Touchdown! Touchdown!" shouted the Cosby kids. "We lead."

Pee Wee felt his heart beating fast. He knew it was time for him to kick the extra point.

"Come on, Pee Wee!" shouted Kathy from the sidelines.

Cluck quacked so hard that he sounded like a flock of ducks all by himself.

Fat Albert held the ball for Pee Wee. Pee Wee ran at the ball and kicked it with all his might. The ball sailed over the goalpost and Pee Wee scored the extra point.

"Attaboy, Pee Wee," shouted Albert happily.

The tough guys made a touchdown on the next play, but Fat Albert's team came right back. The game see-sawed, but Fat Albert's team pulled ahead. The leader of the tough guys paused in the middle of the action and shouted, "Hey, what's the score, man?"

"Forty-four to twenty-three-—*our* favor," announced Pee Wee proudly.

"Guess it's time, then," said the leader.

"Time for what, man?" asked Albert suspiciously.

"Time for our secret weapon!" said the leader. "You turkeys don't stand a chance."

Fat Albert looked at him. He didn't trust that gang leader, but the rest of Fat Albert's gang just laughed.

"Go ahead, turkeys, laugh while you can," said the gang leader. He turned and called down the street. "Okay, Kong, come on out."

The Cosby kids were still laughing when a huge dark shadow slowly fell over them. The laughter stopped.

"Hey!" cried Pee Wee. "What happened to the sun?"

"There must be an eclipse or somethin'!" exclaimed Dumb Donald.

Fat Albert and his gang looked up the street, and
when they spotted what was blocking the sun, their eyes
nearly popped out of their heads. Kong, the tough
gang's secret weapon, was lumbering down the street.
He was a gigantic kid, built like the Hulk. He walked
down the street with all the grace of a woolly mammoth.

The Cosby kids ran behind Fat Albert for protection
as they stared at Kong in awe.

"Gee, he's bigger than you are, Albert," said Pee
Wee.

"Yeah, look at all those muscles," said Bill.

Fat Albert looked down at his belly, which had all the muscle tone of a bathtub full of jelly. Then he looked at Kong. Fat Albert took a deep breath, hitched up his pants, and sucked in his stomach until it became an enormous chest. Now Fat Albert had a shape almost as imposing as Kong's.

"He doesn't scare me," said Fat Albert, holding his breath so that his new "chest" wouldn't disappear.

Kong took a step closer to Albert and growled.

Fat Albert cupped his hand to his ear. "What's that noise?" asked Fat Albert in an innocent tone of voice. "Your stomach?"

Kong pointed at Albert's chest. "Is that yours?" he asked in a low, husky, threatening voice.

Before Fat Albert could answer, Kong poked a finger

into Albert's "chest," and it collapsed, sliding to the ground like an avalanche. It hit the ground and rebounded back to its natural position. The tough gang all laughed so hard they were doubled over.

Albert just glared at them. "Okay, cut the laughin' and let's play!"

Pee Wee placed the ball on the kicking tee—an old tin can. He gave a great kick, but Kong just reached up with an apelike arm and snatched it out of the air. He stood there looking at the ball as if he didn't know what to do with it. Pee Wee stared at him, stunned that anyone had caught his magnificent kick.

The gang leader and a couple of other guys walked up to Kong and simply pointed him in the direction of Fat Albert's goal line. Kong took off in a thundering lope that left footprints in the asphalt. Kong ran through Albert's team as if they were bowling pins. Finally, only fat Albert stood between Kong and the goalpost.

"Here he comes, Albert! Stop him!" Mushmouth yelled.

Fat Albert stood with his legs apart and his arms out in front of him. He looked as tough and mean as he could. "Hey, hey, hey!" growled Fat Albert.

Kong ran into him head-on and just pushed Fat Albert in front of him as if he were a snowplow. The tough gang didn't even bother trying to run interference for Kong. They just sprawled on the sidewalk, their hands behind their heads. The gang leader looked off down the street.

"Stop right there, Kong!" he shouted. "Now touch the ball down!" Kong bent over, touched the tip of the ball to the pavement, and looked back at the leader, beaming proudly.

"Hey, hey, hey," Fat Albert said softly. "I don't know what to say."

"Are you all right?" asked Pee Wee worriedly.

"Yeah," said Fat Albert uncertainly. He got up and shook himself off. He looked around at the Cosby kids, who seemed to have defeat written on their faces.

"Come on, gang," said Fat Albert. "He's not going to stop us."

Chapter Four

SHORT IS BEAUTIFUL

Fat Albert was wrong. One by one, Kong practically destroyed each player on Fat Albert's team. Bruised and almost willing to admit defeat, they gathered for a huddle. Not only had Kong brought his team back from behind, they had gone ahead by a touchdown.

"Anybody got an idea?" said Fat Albert wearily.

"Yeah," said Russell. "Call in the Marines."

"We need a Sherman tank," said Bill. "Maybe, *maybe* that'll stop him."

"I got a better idea," said Rudy. "Let's call it quits. I ache all over."

Fat Albert's face sank. "Maybe we should take a vote," said Fat Albert. "All those who want to quit raise their hands." Everyone just looked at each other. Then, slowly and sheepishly, Bill stuck up his hand, and then Rudy, Weird Harold, Russell, Bucky, Dumb Donald, and Mushmouth. Fat Albert put up his own hand. He looked around. Everyone had his hand up except Pee Wee.

"What's wrong with you?" complained Rudy to Pee Wee. "Do you like being hurt?"

"He hasn't touched me," explained Pee Wee. "I don't think he's even seen me yet. Look, I know why you guys want to quit, and I don't blame you, but I've been thinking, and I've got an idea that just might work. When they get the ball, Kong just stands at the goalpost like a giant and they throw it to him. If I hide under his legs, I might be able to sneak in and get the ball!"

Fat Albert looked at Pee Wee with new respect. Pee Wee was talking differently from the way he usually did.

"Hey, hey, hey," said Fat Albert. "What do you say, guys?"

Russell slapped Pee Wee. "For a little guy, you've got a lot of guts. If you're willing to risk being stepped on by Kong, I'll try to block for you."

"Me too," said the other kids.

Fat Albert and the gang ran out of their huddle. As had become usual, Kong just snatched the ball away from them. Then it was time for the tough gang's team to run their play. Pee Wee ran down the field, trying to keep in the shadows. This was easy, because Kong's shadow was so huge.

The leader of the tough guys' gang threw the ball high to Kong. Pee Wee leapt out from underneath Kong's legs and caught the ball. Kong stared at him with astonishment as if he couldn't understand where Pee Wee had come from.

"Stop him!" cried the leader of the tough gang, but Pee Wee darted and buzzed like a mosquito bound for glory. He crossed the goal line and collapsed, out of breath.

"You did it! You did it!" yelled Fat Albert. "Tie score! Tie score!"

"Not yet!" snarled the leader. "You haven't scored the extra point yet."

"My man Pee Wee never misses," bragged Fat Albert, helping Pee Wee to his feet. "You won't miss, will you?" whispered Fat Albert.

Pee Wee shook his head. He got ready to kick the extra point, but just as the ball was about to sail over the crossbar, Kong reached up his enormous hand and swatted the ball with all his might.

It took off with the sound of a jet plane, sailing way over everyone's head. It hit the wall of a heavily boarded condemned building, took a crazy bounce, and shot right into a small, ragged hole.

"We win!" shouted Kong happily.

The tough gang leader turned on Kong angrily. "Hey, what'd you do that for? That ball is *lost*! I mean gone!"

Kong looked baffled. "You told me to stop him from getting the extra point."

"Don't blame him," said Fat Albert. "He's been doin' all your work for you anyhow."

"You don't dig it," said the gang leader, no longer sounding very tough. "That ball belongs to my big brother. If I lose it, he's gonna really whip up on me."

Fat Albert and the gang went to inspect the hole. It was extremely tiny. In fact, it looked just large enough for a football.

"What am I gonna do? I'm gonna be killed," said the leader.

"Take it easy," said Fat Albert. "Cluck will get it for you!"

"Cluck? Who's Cluck?" asked the gang leader impatiently.

"Cluck is our pet duck," explained Albert.

Cluck waddled out of the stands and over to the hole.

"A duck!" said the leader, sounding disgusted. "Don't jive me, man. I gotta get that ball outa there fast!"

Fat Albert patted Cluck on the head. "Cluck will help you out," he said. "Cluck, go get the ball."

Cluck tossed his beak high in the air. Then he threw out his chest and strutted up to the hole.

But when he got right up there, he looked down the hole, and at the last second he stopped. His beak brushed away a spider web. He peered into the blackness of the hole.

"Hey, Albert," jeered one of the tough gang. "Looks like your duck turned out to be a chicken!"

Cluck marched purposefully and bravely into the opening of the hole. He disappeared.

Pee Wee, Albert, Kathy, and all the other Cosby kids exchanged worried looks. There was a thick silence. Then suddenly the sound of frightened quacks shattered the silence.

Pee Wee fell on all fours and tried to see into the hole. Albert stood next to him. "Can you see anything?" Albert asked urgently. "What's wrong with Cluck?"

"His foot is caught on something and he can't move," said Pee Wee, sounding alarmed.

"Oh no!" cried Kathy. "Poor Cluck!"

"Never mind that stupid duck!" said the gang leader. "I gotta get my brother's ball. Kong, do something." The gang leader shoved Kong toward the hole. Lying flat on the ground, Kong could only put one eye to the hole. He tried pulling at the concrete surrounding the hole, but even Kong couldn't break concrete.

"It's no use!" mumbled Kong.

"It can't be," cried the leader. He started to crawl into the hole, but got in only as far as his neck.

"Hey, I'm stuck," he cried. "Get me outa here. I can't move."

All the guys on his team lined up behind their leader, their hands around each other's waists, and they started tugging. But the gang leader's head stayed stuck in the hole.

One of their gang members looked around. "Don't just stand there, Kong! Give us a hand."

Kong stepped in at the end of the line and put his arms around the last guy's waist.

"Heave ho!" shouted Kong. He yanked with all his might, and the leader popped free, tumbling the whole gang backwards with a big crash.

The leader sat on the ground, holding his head. "Man, there ain't anybody small enough to get in that little hole! My brother's ball is gone forever. I might as well get outa town fast!"

From inside the hole came the sound of a sad quack.

"We can't leave Cluck in there to starve," cried Kathy.

"Hey, Pee Wee," said Albert. "I bet you could get through the hole."

"I dunno, Albert," said Pee Wee. "That hole looks awful small."

"C'mon, man, you can do it," said Bill.

Pee Wee tried to see through the hole. He could hear more frightened quacks coming from Cluck.

"Okay, Cluck," Pee Wee said with determination. "I'm coming in to help you." Pee Wee got down on his knees and started to crawl into the hole.

One of the nastier members of the tough gang started to make a joke. "Man, you *are* making me hungry," he said sarcastically. "First ya send in a chicken and now you're sendin' a shrimp."

The gang leader turned on him angrily. "Cool it," he snapped. "This isn't funny, man." His gang instantly stopped laughing. They all stared at the hole, waiting anxiously.

For several minutes there was no sign of Pee Wee. Then there was a flurry of excited quacks, and Cluck bounded out of the hole and leapt into Kathy's arms.

"Cluck!" cried Kathy happily. "You're all right. You're not hurt."

Fat Albert moved over to make sure Cluck was all right, and Cluck jumped into Fat Albert's arms.

"Nice goin', Pee Wee,'" shouted Fat Albert.

"Hey, where *is* Pee Wee?" asked Dumb Donald.

Bill dropped to his hands and knees and yelled into the hole. "Pee Wee?" Bill's voice echoed back at him, but there was no sound from Pee Wee.

"I hope *he's* not hurt," said Fat Albert anxiously.

"Something could have fallen on him and knocked him out," said Kathy worriedly.

Fat Albert pushed his face against the hole. "Hey, man," he shouted. "Pee Wee! Are you all right?" Still no answer from Pee Wee.

Suddenly the football bounced out of the hole, and seconds later Pee Wee stuck his head out of the hole. "I'm fine," said Pee Wee, grinning. "Just had to go back for the ball."

The leader grabbed the ball and clutched it to his breast. Then he held out his hand to give Pee Wee a "soul slap." "Pee Wee," said the leader, "you are really cool. I ain't ever gonna make fun of you little dudes again. Short is beautiful, man!"

The leader looked over at Fat Albert, who was grinning from ear to ear with pride for Pee Wee.

" 'Course," said the leader disparagingly, "that doesn't go for fat guys."

Fat Albert's smile instantly drooped.

"See ya later," sneered the leader, "*Fat* Albert!" The leader and the gang walked down the street, laughing.

Pee Wee looked up at Albert. "Don't mind them, Albert. You got yourself ten of the best friends in the world!"

Albert looked around at his buddies, from Pee Wee to Weird Harold to Kathy and Cluck. Suddenly he took a deep breath and with a big grin yelled to the heavens . . .

"Hey, hey, hey!"

NOTE FROM BILL COSBY

Looks like my man Pee Wee is walkin' a lot taller now, even though he hasn't grown an inch. I guess it just proves that you can be short and still measure up to the bigger dudes in every other way—and sometimes even *outdo* them. It's something to remember.

MS READ-a-thon—
a simple way to start youngsters reading

Boys and girls between 6 and 14 can join the MS READ-a-thon and help find a cure for Multiple Sclerosis by reading books. And they get two rewards — the enjoyment of reading, and the great feeling that comes from helping others.

Parents and educators: For complete information call your local MS chapter. Or mail the coupon below.

Kids can help, too!

Mail to:
National Multiple Sclerosis Society
205 East 42nd Street
New York, N.Y. 10017
I would like more information about the MS READ-a-thon and how it can work in my area.

Name _____
(please print)
Address _____
City _____ State _____ Zip _____
Organization _____

1—80